fractured

FRACTURED LIT VOLUME 5

Copyright © *Fractured Lit*, 2026. A Red Mare Press book.

Published in partnership with *Fractured Lit*, an online literary journal.

All rights reserved.

No part of this publication may be reproduced or reprinted without prior written permission of *Fractured Lit*. To inquire about rights and reprint permissions, please contact *Fractured Lit*.
www.fracturedlit.com / contact@fracturedlit.com

Red Mare Press upholds the right to free expression and recognizes the importance of copyright in fostering creativity. Copyright exists to inspire writers and artists to produce works that contribute to and shape our culture.

Stories selected by Tara Isabel Zambrano.

Edited by Tommy Dean.

Cover design by Emelie Mano.

Interior design by Cynthia Young and Julianne Johnson.

Red Mare Press / Discover New Art, LLC
70 SW Century Drive, Suite 100442, Bend, Oregon 97702

www.redmarepress.com

Red Mare Press is a division of Discover New Art, LLC.
The Red Mare Press name and logo are trademarks of
Discover New Art, LLC.
The publisher is not responsible for websites (or their content) that are not owned by the publisher.

ISBN 979-8-9939024-0-1

Printed in the United States of America.

fractured

volume 5

contents

Introduction vii

1   Wife 2.0, *Nancy Alvarado* 1

2   Jigsaw, *Anna Cabreros* 5

3   Christina, *Madison Cyr* 9

4   One Day in December, My Trapezius Decided to Write a Short Epic Poem, *Jomil Ebro* 13

5   Nest, *Genevieve Eichammer* 17

6   Blossoming, *Claire Gallagher* 21

7   Dog Years, *Deborah J. Hunter* 27

8   Scintilla River & A Boy Under Glass, *Ariana-Sophia Kartsonis* 31

9   Good Dog, *Karin Kohlmeier* 35

10   Another Friday, *Buddfred Levi* 39

11   Weed, *Beth Cho Little* 43

12   Blackberry Pie, *Kay Nguyen* 47

13   Sick Day, *Kalpita Pathak* 51

14   Kintsugi, *Sascha Sizemore* 55

15   The Bride Is Eating Cake and the DJ Is Playing Werewolves of
     London, *Andrew Stancek* 59

16   Birds, *Laura Theis* 63

17   A Richter Scale for Heartbreaks, *Lynn Kristine Thorsen* 69

18   Empty Bottle, *Joseph V. Velaidum* 73

19   Didn't We Realize We Were Drowning?, *Linda Wastila* 77

20   Hands, *Deb Waters* 81

introduction

Every morning when I raise the window blinds, the sunlight faintly makes its way into my eyes and a myriad of things go through my head, amongst which an idea for a story that sometimes gets on paper—if only a few words—and transforms my day. Over the years, I have realized the power of a story. Like a seed packed with life and meaning, enhancing my understanding of living. Flash fiction is one such form: compact and pulsing with life. Every breath is lucid, injured, or intoxicated with hope.

Here are twenty stories whose common claims are in constantly negotiating contradictions and coming together in fiction that looks back with longing and looks ahead with desire.

I thank Tommy Dean for giving me this opportunity to select final stories for this *Fractured Lit* flash anthology. It was a difficult task to pick some from a collection of unique and dazzling works, each one connecting with me in a different way, but I am glad I had the chance to savor all.

Be prepared to pause and reflect when you come across lines like:

Now no longer small and fierce, she is forever contained, reduced to a box of ash tucked into the recesses of your closet, bones and teeth and memories.

Or the sharp imagery of this:

When we invited the police officer inside that night, I had nowhere to put my nervous energy but the puzzle.

And the beautiful contrast of the inner and outer worlds here:

The world outside was so bright and cold and sure of itself that I hung around in the lobby for a bit just to gather courage.

I hope you feel connected to these stories as I did. Short, powerful bouts of grieving and wonder, as flash fiction should be, interconnected in their search for reality, sending out pieces of the world as they experience it.

TARA ISABEL ZAMBRANO is an award-winning writer of South Asian descent. Her multigenre writing has appeared in *Tin House Online, Electric Literature, Southeast Review, Post Road,* and other notable venues. She is also the author of a short story collection, *Ruined a Little When We Are Born* (Dzanc Books, 2024), and *Death, Desire, and Other Destinations* (Okay Donkey Books, 2020). Find out more at taraisabelzambrano.com and @tizambrano on Instagram.

1

Wife 2.0

NANCY ALVARADO

I.

"Do you want a bite, Linda?" you call out cheerfully from the living room. You're settled into your recliner, hunched gleefully over a cinnamon roll. I pause, grip the broom hovering over a pile of debris in the middle of our tiny kitchen floor. I wanted to playfully scold you for the decadence of the cinnamon roll, but her name falls into the space between us.

I am not Linda.

She was a force, a tiny package of brains and courage. Her presence filled a room. Years before I knew I would love you, I wept at her funeral.

Now no longer small and fierce, she is forever contained, reduced to a box of ash tucked into the recesses of your closet, bones and teeth and memories.

Linda is your dead wife. I choke on her name as I would choke, dry-mouthed, on the cinnamon roll, on the ashes.

The black box from the mortuary takes up more space than its size.

II.

"Sweetie, can you bring me the pictures from the top of the bookcase?"

You call me "sweetie" now, perhaps afraid of how her name and mine intertwine in your mouth, pleasing neither of us.

It's good that I don't believe in ghosts; poster-sized canvases, photos from Linda's memorial service, cascade down on me from the top of the bookshelf where I dared to pull the corner of a frame. Her face, repeated, rains down on my head. Your face, kissing her temple, bruises me.

You are cleaning, purging, heaping a pile of your old life in the middle of the garage. The floor is covered with junk and memories. I silently hand you the stack of photos, gazing one last time into her piercing blue eyes. You gently turn the top photo over, leaving me staring at white canvas, and tenderly place the canvases alongside the broken vacuum cleaner, the plastic bags of expired ginger candy gifted to us almost daily by the neighbor with Alzheimer's, and the leash for a dog who no longer exists. I covertly slide notebooks filled with her spidery writing into the heap, hoping her words will no longer take up so much space in our home.

I keep her journal hidden in our bedroom; I haven't finished reading it.

Two fat men in a truck come to collect the pile. Grunting and sweating, they cart away your old life. I reassure you that you don't have to do this, that you can keep bits and pieces of her until you're ready to let go.

Your reply is brusque. "I know. I'm ready." And then, softly, "Thank you." I touch your shoulder.

I still the urge to beg the two fat men to load their truck faster, to take her away, to let us live as a pair instead of a trio.

III.

You choose a sunny day to let her go. Hard things are always better on sunny days.

I walk silently beside you. For once, I don't want to know what you're thinking. Sand and shells crunch under my feet. I let the sound fill the space between us.

I watch your back, its shape as familiar to me as my own hands, as you step into the water. Foam laps at your knees. You dip your hand into the open bag of Linda's ashes and toss them into the sea.

The wind whips your second handful into the air toward the shore, toward me. Gritty ash lands on my bare arms; I shiver.

Will I always be coated with her residue?

I lick my finger, salt and ash. A wave rises, washing Linda's ashes from my skin.

The sea quietly carries her away, as you turn and walk toward me.

NANCY ALVARADO began her career as an author at age four, when she scratched the word "house" into the wall of her freshly painted house. Her more recent work has been met with less dismay. Nancy holds both a BA and an MFA in writing. She worked for several years as a columnist for the *Chula Vista Star-News*, winning awards for Excellence in Journalism from the San Diego Press Club, the California Reading Association, and the Greater San Diego Reading Association. Nancy's fiction has been previously published in *Relief Journal*, San Diego State University MFA Anthology, *Santa Clara Review*, *A Year in Ink,* the Mason Jar Press *Jarnal,* the San Diego Decameron Project Anthology, and *LatinoLA "Expresate!"* She was one of the Honorable Mention winners in the Writing Away Refuge First Chapter Contest.

$$2$$

Jigsaw

ANNA CABREROS

My sister Jane and I make the ideal jigsaw puzzle partnership. She's more organized than me, the one who categorizes and compartmentalizes, but I have all the patience.

Most recently, we tried a 1,000-piece train travel scene. She dutifully separated the pieces into little groups—landscape, tray of food, luggage, maps. And then there are always those pieces that color-match but blend amorphously into the backdrop—the wall, the shadows, the seat cushions.

I will obsess over fitting these mundane pieces together. But Jane hates the slog. So she focused on the tray of food and the maps as I toiled through the pieces that all looked pretty much alike.

When we invited the police officer inside that night, I had nowhere to put my nervous energy but the puzzle. I'm sure the officer wondered how I could focus on a puzzle amidst a crisis. But I couldn't make myself stop. I felt the disoriented need to be constructive even as I knew nothing I did would change a thing.

"I'm going to ask you some questions. I have to ask them to everyone even though I already have the details of tonight."

"Okay," said Jane.

I rotated a bluish, blurry piece and tried to fit it to another. No luck, no matter the angle.

"Has he ever hit you before tonight?"

"No," she said.

"Has he ever choked you?"

"No."

"Does he have a weapon?"

"Yes."

"Has he ever threatened to kill you?"

"No."

How much has this questionnaire changed since we were kids? I wondered. Did it even exist back then? I thought of how varying the answers would have been depending on the timeline.

As the officer rattled off more questions, I kept trying the pieces. Sometimes looking for matching colors, sometimes honing in on the particular curvature of each edge. I had a few successes, but spent most of my time relentlessly rotating the shapes in hopes of finding them a home.

After the questionnaire was finished, the officer handed my sister a piece pink paper.

"This is an information sheet with numbers to call if you need a safe place to be until we issue the arrest and the EPO. But it looks like you'll stay here, with your sister?"

"Yes," she said.

"That's great," said the officer. "Most women in this situation don't have a safe place to go. You're very fortunate."

Yes, we agreed. Very fortunate.

The officer left, and I kept working the puzzle as Jane calmed herself down. We wondered if her husband would open the door to the police tomorrow since he had refused tonight. If maybe he was too drunk to have heard the police knock tonight. We wondered, when did it get this bad? How hadn't she seen this coming?

She thought she knew him, she said. She knew he was being erratic and increasingly seemed violent, but she never thought he would take it to this extreme.

I was still worrying the pieces when Jane asked if I thought she should go ahead and get him arrested.

"I don't know," I said, pulling apart two mismatched pieces ferociously clinging together. "I would. But it's not my life."

My husband chimed in. "He doesn't know how to control himself," he said reasonably. "Call. It might be the only thing to de-escalate the situation."

He was right, of course. And it was the only thing she hadn't tried. It's the one thing our mother never did.

We set up the air mattress in our youngest daughter's room. On most weekends, she likes to bunk with her older sister. Jane smiled at the small sleeping forms gilded by the nightlight in the adjacent room. She gave me a tender look before retiring to the air mattress.

By the time she was settled, it was nearly 3 a.m. But I wasn't tired. I lay in bed until I heard my husband's breathing regulate, and then I returned to the dining room table.

Jane was there, trying to make sense of the pieces I had set aside. All of them were in the same family of blurry blue, but on closer look, they belonged to completely different parts of the picture.

"I can't sleep," she said. "I thought this would help."

I nodded in agreement and acknowledged that I was there for the same reason.

"But I hate this part of the puzzle," she said. "All the good stuff is done, and now every piece looks the same. It's giving me anxiety, trying to sort it out."

And for the first time that night, tears. She had held it together the entire time, from the moment he slammed her against the wall to the panicked moments on the phone with me, from escaping her house to making it to mine, from calling the police to being questioned by them. All of it had gone so quickly, almost calmly. But now it was over and we weren't sure what was next and she had to decide whether or not she should have her husband arrested the next morning.

I held her and let her cry for a while. Then coaxed her back to bed.

As I walked back through the dining room, I glanced at the nearly finished puzzle. It was true. All the pretty parts of the puzzle were fully assembled, and what was left looked like a monochromatic mess. Big open spaces between the landscape and the tray of food and the luggage and the maps. White space littered with tiny odd shapes, all clearly belonging to each other in some way. But what a process, what a mundane and tedious and painful challenge it was to anchor the beauty to the murky background.

ANNA CABREROS writes fiction and creative nonfiction, focusing on how life's daily beauties, struggles, and mysteries intersect with memory, bending reality and revealing stubborn truths. She lives in Virginia Beach, VA, in her childhood neighborhood with her husband, two children, and a geriatric, probably bionic pit bull.

3

Christina

Madison Cyr

I named her Christina. She began as they all did—a greasy secretion that shimmered and then solidified into a milky coat of wax. It reminded me of the hospital where we were only allowed to write with crayons because you couldn't puncture someone's larynx with a crayon. I spent my time there in the TV room with a box of Crayolas. I peeled off their labels and skinned their naked bodies with my fingernails. I did the same thing to Christina, leaving little white curls of her at my feet.

If not for the hospital, we never would have met.

I saw the poster on my way out. I delivered my discharge paperwork to the reception desk, where the friendly blonde nurse who had admitted me two weeks before was working.

"Feeling better?" she asked. Her tone was so upbeat, I didn't want to disappoint her.

"Much," I said. That made her smile. She told me to have a wonderful day.

The world outside was so bright and cold and sure of itself that I hung around in the lobby for a bit just to gather courage. There was a community bulletin board near the sliding doors, and that's where I saw it.

CLINICAL TRIAL – PAID
Looking to lose 50 pounds or more? You could be eligible to participate in a paid clinical trial for Vitalex.

Maybe I would want to kill myself less if I lost fifty pounds.

THEY TOLD ME it would happen, but still, it was a shock. The wax thickened and hardened. It fell in warm clumps where my joints met. They asked me to collect as much as I could. I saved the clumps and scrapings in dated plastic containers that I refrigerated and delivered to the lab at my weekly check-ins.

At the end of the trial, they gave me my check and asked if I wanted to keep my "production" now that they had no use for it. The trial lasted six weeks. No one ever said the word "fat."

She weighed in at fifty-four pounds. The day I took her home, I searched for "Vitalex Production" on TikTok.

A skinny man in some seaside village sat beside a behemoth mound of yellow tallow. It glistened in the sunlight. He called it Davi and ran his palm over its wet back. Something in his expression touched me. A private smile lifted his lips. His eyes were soft and watery. He opened his hand so wide, splaying all his fingers out, like he couldn't get enough.

I looked at my tub of gray production and grimaced. It wasn't a good look for her, the five-gallon storage bin. And she needed a name. I named her Christina because of the obvious religious parallels. Immaculate conception and all that, and the fact that my own name is Mary.

I bought her an aquarium and wrote messages on the outside with those markers people use to write on car windows:

You're beautiful.

Welcome to the world! It sucks.

My mood lifted. It was good to have somebody to talk to.

A week in, and there was a smell. A cross between earwax and the inside of a belly button. I kept a cinnamon candle burning all day, and that seemed to do the trick.

After a month, the mold appeared in little green freckles across her sallow face. Something had to be done. It was the right thing to do, the only thing to do. I had to take her back.

I'd made Christina over the course of a decade. A few pounds every year, most of it in the past eighteen months when nothing stirred my appetite except ice cream. I bought it in gallon tubs and attacked it with a spoon every few hours. It took time to make her, and it would take time to remake her. The idea was both frightening and a comfort. I missed and was repelled by my old body. But this new body presented its own set of challenges. Even though I was smaller, I found it harder to hide. Men's eyes were everywhere—as omnipresent as the sun or the sky, another element that could kill you from exposure.

I put her in everything. Fried eggs in the morning, a scoop stirred into my coffee where the fat would rise to the top and form an iridescent film. I plopped spoonfuls of her into empty Cool Whip containers and set them out for the stray cats. But it wasn't enough. I needed more mouths.

Misty was the only person I could think of. We'd exchanged info in the hospital, careful numbers copied down in red crayon. She was thrilled.

I made a feast. Two dozen buttermilk biscuits, brown butter gnocchi with fried sage, and a spice cake with buttercream frosting. Enough for us both to feed off the leftovers for days. I didn't hide Christina or make any effort to conceal her role in the meal, and Misty didn't seem to mind. One might say it brought us closer. When I hugged her, I said to myself, "I love you, Misty. I love you, Christina."

It took a month. On our last morning together, I drank my coffee slowly. By then, Christina had a warm, earthy taste, like morel mushrooms. When the coffee was gone, I scraped the sides of her tank with a spatula and set the remains out for the cats. It was a cool spring morning, the dew shone silver on the grass. The cats were waiting for me, their fur shiny and clumped with grease. They wrapped their stout bodies around my ankles and let me scratch behind their ears. When they'd licked the bowl clean, they looked up at me with sorrowful, expectant eyes. I held out my empty hands.

～

MADISON CYR is a fiction writer based in Southern Indiana. She has an MFA in fiction from the Warren Wilson Program for Writers. Her fiction has appeared in *Carve Magazine*, *Leon Literary Review*, and elsewhere.

4

One Day in December, My Trapezius Decided to Write a Short Epic Poem

Jomil Ebro

during a fifty-minute massage. The grading, the emails, the sunken cold: my mid-back balled into a walnut. At Hand and Stone, a blind masseuse named Homer leads me to a room with prancing emerald lights: hospital sink, mirror from Marshalls—a franchised underworld.

"Nice name. Homer. Like the writer," I confirm.

"Like Homer Simpson," he corrects, voice as soothing as the guitar-plucking on Spotify.

Homer's good. I feel his fingers vibrate; riverstone of elbow, railway of forearm, twinge of hidden bruise. But it's the lonely, long vowel of Homer's name that drops me: Hom-er… Home. This time, it's my dad. When he taught me how to hit a homer. Elbows in on the swing. When he'd take me to Home Depot, which I hated because it meant resurrecting a car or a brittle house—I still smell him in 2x4s, see the sun in the tawny of his arm. When he'd say, "Back home in the Philippines…" and the black wind of his eyes curled back somewhere. When he went to EMT school at forty and tried, he got good at naming muscles: rhomboid, soleus. When last we walked on Santa Monica Pier, salted crab in the air, in his maroon Members Only jacket, eating cotton candy just to hold something, I asked in anger why he did that to Mom, and who is my half-sister, and why he couldn't quit smoking so that he might see his grandson be born. When all he'd say was, I know, in that undammable voice which made the gloaming ocean freeze.

O, how I aged into a slender axe that could shatter that Pacific with a lone syllable. How one camouflaged siren of memory beaches us. How I want to approach him, cupping my palms around his trembling matchstick one last time.

～

JOMIL EBRO lives in Golden with his wife and eleven-year-old son. He is a non-dual poet and scholar who identifies as AAPI, and he is a professor at Arapahoe Community College. His PhD is in English and Consciousness Studies. He has received training at the Writer's Workshop at the University of Iowa and degrees in Cultural Studies and Communication at New York University. His poetry and critical essays have been published in *Bath Flash Fiction Anthology, Vol. 7* (Winter 2024), *New Feathers Anthology* (Spring 2024), *Progenitor Literary Journal* (Spring 2024), *Cobra Milk* (Fall 2020), the *Modern Horizons Journal*

(June 2018 and June 2012), the *Journal of Humanities and Cultural Studies Vol. 3, Issue 2* (February 2018), and *Peripheral Matters Journal* from the City University of New York (CUNY, Fall 2017).

5

Nest

Genevieve Eichammer

"The birds are always watching," Mama used to say. We had a bird cage in nearly every room of the house. The parakeets in the living room seemed more at home than I did. The lovebirds in the kitchen reminded everyone how bonded they were every time you tried to make dinner. The dining room was free of her pets, with the intention of not making guests uncomfortable. Mama could not accept that we never had guests. Her taxidermied finch found its place in my bedroom, right on the windowsill. When I was younger, I tried to make it fly out of the window a number of times, but it always found its way back inside. The dead ones were always replaced, even if they could not be found. The smell of our bungalow in the summer heat was pungent even from down the road.

Mama's room was the worst. The canaries rarely remained in their cages and would flutter uncontrollably around the room. The sick ones would slam themselves into everything. The bursts of bright yellow and orange were never-ending. "My stars," she would say dreamily, as she admired them bouncing between the walls.

For my sixth birthday, as many children have, I asked for a dog. She cackled for days, weeks. Instead, I received a kiss on the cheek and a brand new bicycle. "When you're all grown up, you can have a dog in your house," she told me. I grew up, got a job, and applied to college. Zero acceptances. No dog. I stayed home and took care of aging Mama. The chain-smoking, combined with the stench of our home, left her coughing all day long. Mama never went to the doctor, but you could tell she was sick. The ringing in my ears was incessant, as was the hacking from Mama, and the chirping from the birds. For years, my coworkers, friends, and the occasional romantic partner, insisted that I move out. But they didn't understand. There was no one left to care for her.

On one of her bedridden days during a harsh winter, Mama begged me to clean the cage of the parakeets. She could not confess that they had not been cleaned in years, but rather pleaded with me to have mercy on the birds. I brought each bird to her room, one by one, letting them free on her chest. The fourth and final parakeet nudged itself into her neck. She cooed at them, petting them eagerly and showing incredible newfound strength as I shut the door behind myself.

The cage was better than expected. There was only one set of remains nestled away in the corner, which I scooped into a shoe box for Mama. She liked to keep all of her pets. The soiled paper stacked at the bottom was glued into place and only came free after chipping away at the sides with a butter knife. Mama insisted on using newspaper as a cage liner, as we would never run out.

I could barely make out the date on a chunk directly in the middle, reading September 19, 1999. The smell penetrated my nostrils, but after two and a half decades, it barely phased me. I continued to read the scattered words, dates, and headlines throughout the mucky newspaper. The next fragment had my name on it.

I cleaned each cage in the house and made myself a puzzle. Mama was simply overjoyed that she was surrounded by the birds, trilling with them and caressing them as I worked to decipher the barely legible scraps I collected. After hours of searching, it was complete. "Congratulations! You have been accepted into Michigan State University! Welcome to the Class of 2002."

I told Mama I was going to the store to get more newspapers. "Go on, the birds will take good care of me until you get back." I spent that night at my coworker's house. And the night after. After thirty-two nights of sleeping on his dingy blow-up mattress, I signed the lease on my own apartment.

The call from the sheriff came almost exactly a year later. I was on a campus tour. His voice was firm, grounding. "The deputies found her in her bedroom. Neighbors called about a wellness check. You know, about the smell. They thought it was the pets."

"And the birds?" I questioned.

"Dead too." He cleared his throat before continuing. "And a couple of crows came in through the window after she passed. But don't you worry about that, funeral homes these days can fix things like that right up."

Mama always left her bedroom window open. Her stars never left, but she prayed for new ones to join us and come through there to start their new life in our home. I have joined the Class of 2011 at Michigan State University, and my roommate does not seem to like me, or perhaps it is just my decor. The stiff finch from my childhood bedroom has found a new home in my dorm.

～

GENEVIEVE EICHAMMER is a recent English graduate and writer living in Toronto. Her short story, "Cherry Wine," was published last fall in the *White Wall Review*.

6

Blossoming

Claire Gallagher

The bruises bloom like purple flowers. Hibiscus perhaps. Hibiscus × rosa-sinensis. The marks will fade to a deep blue. Like cineraria. Cineraria senetti. After that, a sickly yellow.

Tansy. Tanacetum vulgare.

You recite the names in your head, your mouth forming soundless words.

A hairline fracture in the ceiling captures your attention. An imperfection in the otherwise immaculate surface. You're surprised he hasn't noticed. Fixed it. Like he tries to fix you.

Lying on the bed that you share, you wonder when he'll be back.

It won't happen again. I swear.

HE LIKES TO drink beer in the sunshine. Today he's watching you plant marigolds.

Calendula officinalis.

"Make sure you don't track dirt into the kitchen again," he says. The bottle clanks as he places it down on the patio table.

You turn your face in his direction. Nod once. In your peripheral vision, you see him stand and stretch.

"I'm going for a nap."

You turn back to your task, listen as his footsteps recede. You breathe in through your nose, out through your mouth.

THE GLASS LIES in fragments on the kitchen floor. You imagine one of them slicing into your finger, the blood that will flow down to your wrist when you hold it up. Rose-red. Deep Secret. Floribunda.

He's at work. You must sweep up the mess before he returns. But you know his lips will tighten when he notices the missing tumbler.

YOUR GOWN IS ankle length with a high neckline. Periwinkle blue. Vinca minor.

You did not want to come to the ball. Did not want to sit here while he bids for expensive lots.

A squeeze of your thigh. Warm breath in your ear. "You'd better not be making eyes at him."

You realise your gaze has been fixed on the man seated opposite while your mind wandered.

A quick response. "No." You focus your attention on your half-finished meal.

You sense him studying your profile. A heartbeat, two, three. Then his lips move to your neck.

"WHEN ARE YOU coming to visit? I haven't seen you for months," your mother says.

Your grip tightens on the phone. "Soon."

You wait for him to arrive home.

When he walks through the door, you keep your gaze on his tie. Black narcissus. Not black, but deep red. You offer your cheek.

"My mother called," you tell him over dinner. "She wants us to visit."

"She called you, or you called her?"

"She called me."

He sighs. "You know how I feel about your parents."

"If we don't go, they might turn up here."

A frown. "I don't want your dad here, stinking out my house with his cancer sticks."

Your father always smokes in the garden, but you don't point this out.

"And your mother looks down on me."

You remain silent.

"Look at me."

You lift your eyes.

"Don't I provide for you?"

You lick dry lips. "Yes."

"Don't I give you everything you could ever want?"

"Yes."

"Am I not good enough for you?"

"You're more than enough."

He stares at you. "Then say it."

"I love you."

YOU JOIN THE queue at the bakery, inhale the yeasty aroma.

Three women sit at a table for four. They sip frothy coffees and share gossip. You remember what that's like, the camaraderie of friendship, the intimacy of exchange.

There are no free tables. You wonder if you could buy a drink, ask to join them.

Pretend that you belong for a while.

Forget-me-not, you want to tell them. Myosotis sylvatica.

You reach the front of the queue, ask for the loaf, examine the drinks menu. Flat white, you are about to tell the young man. But a small commotion draws your attention back to the table. The women are standing, kissing cheeks, promising to meet again soon.

"Anything else?"

You turn back to the server, shake your head.

YOU WILL PACK lightly. Return to your childhood home.

There will be tears, anger. At him, not you. The police will be called. He'll be questioned, held accountable. You can show them the fresh bruises between your thighs.

But he calls the office, says he's sick, spends the day watching you with hooded eyes.

How did you know? you wonder. How did you know?

YOU LOSE TRACK of days and nights. Your world is small, your isolation total. From eight to six, you live in silence, until the rain stops one afternoon and you can return to your garden. Now the birds sing to you. You almost smile.

Geraniums are repotted. Pelargonium graveolens. You like the texture of the furry leaves, the earthy scent. Time becomes meaningless.

Until it isn't.

YOU SELECT A packet blindly and head to the counter. Your hand shakes as you tap your card on the reader. You don't remember the journey home.

It's awkward to hold the stick between your legs while you pee. You finish and place it next to the sink, then sit on the edge of the bath tub and stare at it until it reveals its secret.

Two lines. Pink. Anemone sylphide.

You lurch back to the toilet.

You're still there when he returns. You push yourself up, fumble to hide the test at the back of a cupboard, swill some mouthwash.

"Where are you?"

You press the flush in response. Stare at the mirror as you wash your hands.

Who are you?

THE LADY'S VOICE is reassuring. "We'll develop a plan with you, assign you a bed in one of our refuges. You'll be safe there."

Safe.

When you disconnect the call, you pack minimally and pause to look out of the kitchen window. Your garden is blooming. Perhaps the refuge will have a few flower beds you can nurture.

As you walk down the street, you do not look back.

CLAIRE GALLAGHER is a UK-based former teacher now working for a national charity. She's self-published several contemporary novels and her short stories have been featured in the world's longest running women's magazine. Exploration of both the light and the dark side of humanity appeals to Claire, so she writes both uplifting fiction and that of a more unsettling nature. "Blossoming" and "They Say" reflect her fascination with the latter.

7

Dog Years

Deborah J. Hunter

I was on our excuse for a back porch, no one ever put in screens, and it smelled like oranges under my fingernails. Jack lowered himself into the lawn chair next to the old Boy Scout cot I was on, looking up at the rain-stained roof with bits of tar paper peeking through. Old Spice tapped my nose. The guy loved soap on a rope. He was nineteen and recovering from spine surgery. His sandy hair was matted around his significant ears. I didn't get the details, but he had to go all the way to Syracuse to have the tumor removed.

"You counting nails up there or something?" Jack said.

"Just thinking."

His voice was low like Dad's. Slow like Mom's. He was impatient with lugs like me and my all-time favorite. His current predicament seemed to give him a little more patience. Mom says he walked me around in the Taylor-Tot when I was little.

I asked him once why he did it. "I loved riding in that thing when I was small," he said. "And you liked to go, the word 'go' lit you up like a Christmas tree."

"It's not going to happen, kid," Jack said.

"I can make it happen."

I was going to Woodstock, it was a few hours away by car, and I could get most of the way by bus. I just turned thirteen, and my folks were Hell No about it. It's all I thought about, mostly so I wouldn't think about Jack dying, not that anyone said he would, but nobody said he wouldn't either.

I would take the city bus from our neighborhood to downtown. Last year, while another brother was still in Vietnam, I took it all the way to Utica for an anti-war demonstration. Only twelve other people showed up, and I was the only one in Land Lubbers and Jesus sandals. That getup cost me ten nights of babysitting.

My folks thought the case was closed, my going to that "hippie-dippie weird thing," as my father called it. I didn't argue, counting on what Jack called, "benign neglect." I had already tucked a pair of undies and socks in my book bag and would tell whoever was around on Friday, while the folks were at work, that I was going to the library downtown.

"You good, kid? I am going back in to take a pill and a rest," Jack said like an ancient.

"Yep."

I was scared when I got on that bus to Middletown. The creepy Charles Manson news, the war, and having never been farther than Oneida Lake. I had my map and a copy of *Fire from Heaven*.

Twelve dollars in the right front pocket of my jeans and my return ticket in my bra.

A big, dark-haired girl sat next to me on the crowded coach.

"Where you going?" she said.

She hit the "you" hard, like in a gangster movie. Her eyes were so brown, and they disappeared when she laughed, and she laughed at everything. Like when I told her I was going to Middletown and then to Woodstock, and when the guy behind us asked why anybody from up here would go way down there to hang out with thousands of people who never took a bath.

"How old are you?" she asked.

"Fifteen."

"Not."

I shut up. She was probably only fifteen herself. But she had a different kind of life than me. I could tell she knew stuff, and I already loved her for that.

"How old are you?" I said.

"Fifteen, but it's like in dog years. Why don't you get off with me in Little Falls?"

I got off and we went to her place out in the country, a few miles from the station. Some old man in a pickup met her at the bus and drove us out to the house with faded orange paint peeling like a bad sunburn. The old man left without a word.

"Gramps never says much," she said.

After we ate some chips with onion dip and drank some soda, we got on the bed in her room and talked. Her absent father, my sick brother, her dead horse, and my brother in the war, and the war being in the living room, her mother who is never home and always talking when she is, and saying things a kid shouldn't even hear. We did stuff on that bed, with its quilt worn to the stuffing and stinking of Pall Malls and patchouli. She had slender fingers and no real wrists at the ends of her jelly roll arms. Her grief settled over me like fog on birches.

"I like the angles of you," she said. "I dream of being what Gramps calls 'lanky.'"

"Lanky isn't you, it's nothing special," I said.

Then I wanted to go.

She called Gramps, and we rode back to the station. I got home before dark with my front pocket empty. I forgave her for that; twelve bucks wasn't a lot to spend to get protected from your own silly self. I did some explaining, took my grounding of no buses for two weeks, and went to bed with a nose full of adventure.

That fall I contracted mono in the hospital after having my adenoids out. Jack had another surgery, and somebody brought the cot in from the porch and set it up in the living room next to the couch. We tried to do homework and watched the tube. We ate hot dogs and applesauce for lunch. The Miracle Mets won the World Series that October, which was worse TV than Lawrence Welk for a couple of diehard Yankees fans. I cheered for the Baltimore Robinsons (Frank and Brooks). Jack had bright red seams in his neck and holes in a head that was now held up by a contraption from Dr. Frankenstein's laboratory. There was trouble ahead for the both of us.

⌒

DEBORAH J. HUNTER is a retired technical writer living in Tulsa, Oklahoma. Two pieces from her creative nonfiction collection, *Enchanted Exile*, received awards from *Southwest Writers* and the *Tulsa Library Essay Contest*. The full collection is under agent consideration. She is a Millay Colony for the Arts residency alumna.

8

Scintilla River & A Boy Under Glass

Ariana-Sophia Kartsonis

His body was cocooned in ice. A casket of ice. Like one of those gag gift ice cubes—plastic-clear with a fly trapped in the center. Illinois winter was that plastic cube and he—that boy—miles and years downriver—he was that fly.

He was that fly. If he'd been alive today, that's what the girls might have said. He was a sweet-eyed boy with soft hair and paw-like hands. He came to school that year with a triangle of torso.

Shoulders wider, body shrugging beneath as if the tension of all those years would send sparks to the ends of his fingers. Anyone who touched him surely lurching from the voltage.

Now, on a television screen ten years downstream, he zips by, still a boy, and frozen that way. His last breath is one of the plumes of chalkiness that made the occasional cloud through the clarity. As if, really, a decade dead, he might be in a magician's glass case and breathing away, puffing out smoke-feathers of living breath and fogging up the place.

If that ice were a diamond, that breath would be the flaw.

He was their only boy. Theirs was an odd house and that boy, when we were all just kids, he was always something else. Then he was gone. And that, became the most of who he'd been. The gone boy. The boy without a way back.

The parents moved away the next spring. The boy, by then, unfound, forgotten. We grew up. None of us were his best friend. None of us kissed him. No one knew his favorite color. The name of his dog. But we had all lied about one of these things.

Mine was the kiss. It felt like the truth because he was the pillow I propped on the left side of my canopy bed. He was the ghost I tried to bring back by the light of a strawberry candle and a gathering of plush animals. The makeshift Ouija board I made from cardboard, a pushpin, a construction paper arrow and symbols I copied from hieroglyphs, from Sanskrit and Arabic and any language that seemed mysterious and full of images I didn't understand. It would take all these years and an ailing marriage to know that any language would've worked.

But nothing brought him back. Even when I set my room at twelve years old like a radio dial to host any number of creepy spirits. Even when that fruity candle cast a shaky spell of shadows on the west wall, I never felt his presence. I could terrify myself with those ghostwishing rituals and never once feel the slightest cool wind telling me he was there. His lakely cowhide flask of a form gone liquid in the most vaporous way. Lips still gray from the other world romantically dead and returned to me. I never heard the gurgle of him, mouthful of river, his hair laurelled with twigs and reeds never drizzled river on the impossibly pink carpet. There was nothing but the ritual itself—and like the most rigid faiths that alone sustained it.

Now he was back. The television ran him down that river a hundred times it seemed. Ran my childhood back to me—him there stuck in our twelfth year and me in my bathrobe—the scratchy terrycloth anniversary gift from my ill-fitting husband of four years, and the life I had accepted somehow, it seemed to me, by accident.

Me, pregnant and crying because I still had yet to feel as much as I had the year he vanished, the long dark winter I worshiped his absence, set up churches and séances and learned, maybe too well it seems to me now, how to cling to the vacancies more than the body. I wrote long letters in my journal, worked on making mine the curliest of cursives, my printing whimsical. I wrote of him and true love 4-ever, I wrote of the romance of the dark sorrow of our moth-life love. I understood saints who swooned themselves into ecstacies with their vespers. I prayed that boy back into being. Now he'd come back all wrong, swaddled in ice, glass, the dignity of the dead, but hanging there like a put-away puppet on the TV.

The news said the body had been kept in ice these last ten years, that the boy, with the grace of better freezing and more advanced science, might almost be revived, arriving to the world ten years tardy with no good excuse and cold settled eternally in the marrow of his bones. Or maybe it said only that he'd been frozen alive, one blunt blow to the cranium and then dropped in a deep freeze coffin filled with water and frozen solid.

In diamonds it's called an inclusion or an included crystal—a diamond or a crystal formed inside another. That baguette of ice and the boy suspended and floating in the glass rectangular nowhereness of the television screen. The images multiplying reminding me of an Escher drawing more than my life.

The life it held inside all that glass and ice was not the boy's life anymore but my own losses. Tucked into a threadbare place where once there'd been a shirtpocket I wanted there to be a letter written from the girl I'd been when he'd vanished. A drenched white envelope and inside, a letter in my heart-dotted i, bloated-bubble-letters spelling out just what it was I had once wanted so much. I wanted it to tell me how I hoped to feel about a life on ice, on hold, with a body suspended in my own, and love stopped cold in its tracks.

ARIANA-SOPHIA KARTSONIS, author of *Intaglio*, *The Rub*, and a few chapbooks, lives in Columbus, Ohio.

9

Good Dog

Karin Kohlmeier

Dad calls it "Eyesore Trashtown." I don't read perfect yet, but looking at the letters on the sign, I don't think that's right. "It's called Eastlake Terrace," Mom says, hugging her purse tight and shooing me into the elevator. "Dad thinks he's funny."

Dad wasn't funny this morning, whisper-fighting with Mom, both of them thinking I couldn't hear, as me and her were leaving the house. In the car, I tried to ask her about it, how somebody could spend money they don't have, and what he meant by calling this lady the Snow Queen of Welfare, but Mom's look said shut my hole, so I did.

Now in the elevator, the wobbly box I'm carrying—with cans all on one side and a big box of crackers on the other—makes my arms burn. I distract myself by watching Mom change her face, so by the time the doors open, the line between her eyebrows is gone and she's wearing a big smile.

The lady who opens the door Mom knocks on doesn't look like any kind of queen to me. She has yellow hair like mine on the ends, but where it comes out of her head, it's dark brown. She's wearing a baggy T-shirt and stretchy pants that have holes in the knees. This is an apartment, which is like our house except way smaller and with a bunch of them crammed together in one building. It smells like old cigarettes and some kind of food I'm glad I don't have to eat.

There's a kid about my age—Annie, she says—and Mom tells me to go play. Annie's room has three unmade beds and a dresser. The carpet has stains, and the closet door doesn't close right. We sit on the floor, and Annie hands me a little plastic Snoopy—the kind with a hole in the bottom because it's supposed to go on the end of a pencil. "I love Snoopy!" I say, but Annie says, "Don't call him that." She takes him back and rubs him against her cheek. "His name is Harrison K. Snooples The Third," she says. "You can call him Mr. Snooples." She kisses him and hands him back. I bring him to my nose and sniff. He smells like plastic, strawberry ChapStick, and dirt.

While Annie digs in the closet for more toys for us to play with, I watch Mom and Other Mom unload the groceries in the kitchen—all the cheapest brands, like Mom says, we're going to have to start buying.

"Let's play Barbies," Annie says. She hands me Ken, she's Barbie, and Snoopy is their pet dog. Even though he's way too small to look like their dog for real, Annie takes Barbie's hand and makes it pat his little head. "Good dog, Mr. Snooples," she says. "I love you."

I've been trying out a word I learned from Dad, and I shout it out now as loud as I can: "Imbecile!" I lift Ken's arm and do my best Dad voice: "This imbecile thinks he can lay me off when I gave my heart and soul to that company!"

"Let's kiss," Annie says and smooches Barbie's face into Ken's.

When the kissing is done, I sit Ken down on the floor and put Snoopy on his lap. I make Snoopy go around in a circle three times before he sits down like a real dog. "Good job, Mr. Snooples," I say because I know Annie will like it. She laughs and goes digging in a pile for a new dress for Barbie to change into.

I watch Mom in the kitchen talking with Other Mom. The line in her forehead is starting to come back. In the store earlier, she got a notebook out of her purse and did a bunch of math problems, then she put back the steaks she was buying for our dinner and got a package of hamburger instead. She had promised me Pop-Tarts, but she changed her mind to "maybe next time."

When it's time to go and I stand to leave, Annie asks for Mr. Snooples back. I say, "I gave him back to you. Where did you put him?" and start lifting Barbie clothes, hunting under them for Snoopy. Mom says let's go, and we leave Annie crawling on the floor, flinging aside Barbies and clothes and calling, "Mr. Snooples, where are you?"

In the car on the way home, I take Snoopy out of my pocket. My window is rolled halfway down, and I hold him balanced on the edge of the glass. I lean him in. I lean him out, feeling the wind trying to catch him out of my hand. Then I let go. I crane my neck to watch him bounce in the road until he's crunched under the car behind us.

KARIN KOHLMEIER is a writer and visual artist. She lives in New York City with her cats.

10

Another Friday

Buddfred Levi

Back home inside our first floor apartment at 2 p.m., as we were, after a morning at the city library where we spent several hours while Mom searched through the mysteries for one that suited her and I picked out a couple of graphic novels, after Mom had splashed the leftover bottle of wine from her pantry storage into a large glass to complement a small snack (cream-cheesed everything bagel) from the fridge, and after she sat down at the kitchen table to eat and to write out a list of groceries she wanted for dinner from the local delicatessen which she completed and handed to me, I, sneaking two cigarettes from her purse, set off through the kitchen door, down the stairs to the basement exit, lighted up and smoked one while taking the shortcut through the dirt alleyway which stretched behind rows of apartment complexes from our apartment to a nearby block of stores where the delicatessen was located and where, after entering, I squeezed between a couple of shoppers who were eyeing various foods displayed in refrigerated compartments, handed the list to Isaac who was tending to the counter fronting shelves filled with groceries along the back wall and from which he filled the list, added the total cost to our standing credit account, told me to be careful and handed me the bag which I promptly smashed on the door when I started to exit and a full bottle of Gallo red wine broke and poured down onto the dingy gray linoleum and while Isaac was quick with a mop and broom, the other customers wondered what a young teenager was doing with a bottle of Gallo red wine and I stammered my mother is a gourmet cook to no one in particular and everyone in general and I took the second bottle of wine from Isaac who had, after calling my mother about the bill, rescued the other groceries to which I added the wine and I backed out red-faced and cautiously through the doorway to freedom, hurried home without smoking the second cigarette, yelled "I'm home!" to Mom, dropped off the order on the kitchen table beside an empty glass and a half-eaten bagel, retreated to my room, crawled under my twin bed, grabbed the flashlight I kept handy to read all the comics stored there hidden, and waited for my father to get home from work, hiding from the argument that would follow at the kitchen table over dinner, the yelling and excuses, Father's storming out muttering about a divorce, my mother's tears, and the inevitable snoring as she went to sleep, soon followed by my father's return home and to bed beside her.

BUDDFRED LEVI is an octogenarian living in Wichita, Kansas, and a graduate student at Wichita State University. He has had several stories published in *Mikrokosmos,* and one is online at the *New English Review.*

11

Weed

Beth Cho Little

The sky went dark on a Monday, pushing the straining sun behind a curtain of smoke, creating an opaque swath of grayness where light would catch—lost—never making it to the retina, never lighting up the things we had been used to seeing: tree leaves in the sunlight, a glint off the lake, a squinty view of a deer through the trees, the forest floor spotted and daring looking, and so, in this relative darkness—thick and vast—we see with our hands out in front of us, using them as a guide, a buffer, a shield against a stumble over the rake in the yard, the log in the road, the slick of wet leaves on the front path, our own feet, ourselves—clumsy and fumbling as ever.

It's only been a week since the smoke and its particles put up a blanket across the sky. It's only been a week and, already, I struggle to recall the exact way the sun used to glow through the cluster of birches off the back side of the house, the dark woods backlit behind them. The smoke and the flames have been on the news for months, years. The fires continue to burn and move, overtaking everything, and while they have never been where we are, this time, their effect is inescapable, and one day we woke up to a sky unchanged by morning light, and we wondered but didn't speak our questions out loud. The next night we stayed up to watch the sky, absent of stars, never turning into morning. Then the following night, we stood on the back stoop, waiting to see one single star. Hank grabbed his headlamp and said, "Go to bed. I'll be up in a bit." I watched him from the bedroom window, on all fours, his face close to the ground, studying something, the brightest setting shining from his forehead. I thought I heard a yell in the dark, but I went to bed anyway.

The next morning, I woke to his side of the bed undisturbed and the truck gone from the garage, and now, the sky is dark and the house is empty except for me and the dog, and I work at remembering the way the street looked with the light of an unshadowed sun shining through the branches onto the dirt, brightening the way ahead.

Last week, before the sky went gray, Hank had razed a long section of ground in the yard. He had wielded the machete he bought at the flea market in Brownfield, hacking at a particular green stalk that sprouted in the dark soil. With every swing of the metal, rocks and pebbles—disturbed from the earth—flew all around him with vengeance. The little bits of green—the offenses—threatened the well-being of Hank's beloved roses and blueberry bushes, his tulips and herbs. I could hear him ranting about the roots and sprouts and green bits, how he knew they would choke the life out of the plants he'd chosen, the ones that belonged. As if he knew the world was about to change and there was no way he'd stay and live in it with me and his doomed flora, Hank took the truck and hit the road.

Now, I stand at the edge of the property and turn my light to the brightest setting, checking again to see if what I think I see is true, if growing out of the black dirt—where he had stamped down and beaten back every stem and every green speck with his worn work boots—there are in fact thirty or forty little green shoots a couple centimeters high; the weed is not obliterated; even in the grayness, it is very much alive. And, considering the massacre of leaves and stems, branches and soil that took place here only a week ago, a barely comprehensible and resilient little thing.

My arms are folded against the morning chill, and I hear Hank and his friend Vesta "the Garden Guru" talking a month or so ago—their words cutting through the emptiness of the dark yard: *invasive, not from here, alien.* I see the ways they averted their glances, avoiding my hair—thick and black, long around my shoulders; my eyes—narrow and dark; my skin—olive in the sun, contrasting me with all the whiteness: her, Hank, every neighbor for miles, the shutters on the house. She had spat her words: "That weed is downright stealing the space of what's ours. You know what I mean." I did, and she knew it. And now, watching the little plant push through the soil, I laugh; it bursts from me in the silent woods—a loudness echoing through the trees.

BETH CHO LITTLE has an MLitt with distinction (fiction) from the University of St Andrews in Scotland and an MFA (Writing for Young People) from the Solstice MFA Program of Lasell University. Beth's work has been published in the anthology *Somebody's Child: Stories About Adoption, Eastown Fiction, YARN: The Young Adult Review Network,* and *Hunger Mountain.* She was awarded an SCBWI Magazine Merit Honor in 2016. Her most recent piece of short fiction, "On Falling in Love at Boarding School," won the

2023 Flash Fiction Contest for *Pigeon Pages*, judged by Gina Chung. She attended the Kenyon Review Writers' Workshop in summer 2023 and the Tin House Summer Workshop in 2024.

12

Blackberry Pie

Kay Nguyen

Cora couldn't explain why she was baking a blackberry pie at three in the morning, even though she hated blackberry pie. She couldn't explain why she dug into every cardboard box, searching for all her kitchen tools. She couldn't explain why she tossed everything else aside, leaving the apartment a devastating mess.

Maybe because she'd just moved in a week ago.

Maybe because her mom passed unexpectedly a few days later.

Maybe because she'd spent all day planning her estranged mom's funeral, because her dad was hysterical from the pain.

Maybe it was all of the above.

Cora couldn't explain why she'd spent the last two hours looking for her mom's old handwritten cookbook, tearing frantically through every box in a grief-fueled rage. She couldn't explain why she'd never thrown it out, even though she hadn't used it in almost a decade. She couldn't explain why she kept it, even when her mom cut ties with her after Cora finally had the courage to come out.

Maybe because she couldn't remember if the little hardcover notebook had a pink or red rose on the front.

Maybe because when she'd called all her mom's contacts to notify them, she'd barely recognized half the names.

Maybe because she needed to ensure that page twenty-two wasn't all made up in her head.

Maybe it was all of the above.

Cora couldn't explain why her eyes welled up with tears when she found the cookbook at the bottom of the very last box. She couldn't explain why her heart broke to see the cover stained and scratched, the pages stuck together and torn.

Maybe because it was the only thing she had left of her.

Maybe because of all the strangers who told her how blessed they were to know her mom.

Maybe because all her dad's efforts to reunite them had gone to waste.

Maybe it was all of the above.

Cora couldn't explain why she made the pie with the utmost care—carefully measuring each ingredient and following the recipe word for word. She couldn't explain why she made the crust from scratch and checked every berry for imperfections. She couldn't explain why she painstakingly latticed the dough on top, adjusting until it was absolutely perfect.

Maybe because page twenty-two had Cora's Favorite—Mom's Blackberry Pie written at the top in her mom's beautiful cursive.

Maybe because, as the pie baked, she realized that not all their memories were painful ones.

Maybe because she remembered early mornings waking up to blueberry pancakes and late nights licking the brownie spoon.

Maybe because she never picked up any of her mom's calls that had started coming in just last month.

Maybe it was all of the above.

Cora couldn't explain why she watched the sun rise as she waited for the pie to cool. She couldn't explain why her vision blurred when she realized it looked just like her mom's in the golden morning glow. She couldn't explain why she began to sob after taking the first bite.

Maybe because it was so delicious—tart, gooey, and warm.

Maybe because, long ago, she used to call her mom her best friend.

Maybe because she feared her mom had died, wondering if she still loved her.

Maybe because she never got the chance to tell she did.

Maybe because she realized her mom never stopped loving her either.

Maybe it was all of the above.

KAY NGUYEN is an unpublished author who has recently revived her childhood passion for writing. She is focused on writing her first novel while also dabbling in short story contests. By day, she is a neuroscience researcher living in Seattle with her long-term partner, dog, and cat. In her free time, she enjoys indoor gardening and cozy video games.

13

Sick Day

Kalpita Pathak

Ma keeps Nabh home again because he's still fatigued, and she says he has such heavy bags under his eyes he could go for a month-long trip to India. No fever, though. He's well enough to be bored.

And… he's going to miss the fire drill today. No big whoop, except Mrs. Reyes always gives free time if her students walk in an orderly fashion and stay together during the drill. Nabh and Kyle planned on making a prank video—gluing quarters to the floor and recording people trying to pick them up. He wonders if Kyle will do the prank by himself and get all the likes.

School is down the street from Nabh's apartment. He hears the 7:55 bell ring while he's curled on the couch with Krishna watching Unspeakable on YouTube. Nathan Graham is Nabh's hero; he barely notices when Ma kisses him goodbye.

After a late breakfast—Nabh's classmates have already started writing—Ajoba does the dishes and sweeps the floor, moving stiffly, hunched over with age. The skin on his hands is thin, bleeding in a couple of spots from washing. Nabh feels so guilty. Ajoba is old. He's supposed to sip tea on the balcony, not clean and cook for his nine-year-old grandson.

Then Ajoba smiles at Nabh. "If you can't go to school, you can at least further your education by reading." His sparkling eyes are deep set, surrounded by brown, wrinkly skin that drapes around them like the dhoti he wears when he does his asana.

Nabh needs no convincing. Ajoba clips a leash on Krishna, and slowly they walk to the library: an old man, a sick boy, and a rescue dog who marks his spot every few steps.

They push through the library doors at ten o'clock. His classmates are doing reading now, just like Nabh's about to. Cosmic Symmetry, Ma would call it. Krishna pulls Ajoba to the front desk, where the librarian keeps a jar of Milk-Bones. Nabh disappears in the stacks.

After checking out their books, Ajoba suggests they read in the park. It's a warm morning, sun glowing, dew on the green grass long evaporated. A couple of minutes in, and Ajoba is snoring, drool glistening in the corner of his mouth, book rising and falling on his chest. Krishna's on his back, tongue lolling out, eyes rolled up so only the whites show.

"Ew." Nabh giggles.

An empty school bus stops at the intersection before turning right toward school, two blocks away. The hiss of the airbrakes reminds Nabh of steam pushing out of Ajoba's teakettle. He turns the page of his Percy Jackson book, startling when Ajoba starts talking in a sleep-husky voice.

"The shapes you see in clouds are possessions people leave behind when they die." His eyes are opaque and inscrutable as he stares at the sky. "Ghosts of possessions." Nabh puts his book down and inspects the sparse clouds. A rabbit, ears raised high. A leaping dolphin. An orange tree. No possessions.

"Not every shape, of course. But some." Ajoba holds out a little packet of dried amla.

Nabh chews on the tart, salted gooseberries while he decides if Ajoba is teasing. This is, after all, the man who smashed a spider with a frying pan last night and pretended to cook it for Nabh's dinner, both of them laughing so hard they couldn't breathe while Ma threw her hands in the air, a smile breaking through the exhaustion on her face.

The bell rings for the end of morning kindergarten, and Nabh imagines the little kids climbing the steps of the awaiting bus, small hands grasping the handlebars to help hoist them up. The day is going by so much more quickly than it does when he's actually in school. Pretty soon, the bell will ring for the upper grades to have lunch.

"Lunch," growls Nabh's stomach. He's definitely feeling better because he's really hungry for the first time in days. And he gets to eat sweets because he's sick! Maybe today he can get a chocolate milkshake from Bomb Burger.

Before Nabh can ask, Ajoba clears his throat. "When my ma expired from breast cancer, I was a little older than you. Her bed was by the window, and I saw in the clouds her bangles, my lattu spinning as if it were on the table, a heart."

Now Nabh thinks he also sees a heart, but it breaks in two, the pieces separating, elongating until they're nothing more than wisps of clouds. A tear falls from Ajoba's eyes and runs down his temple. Definitely not teasing.

Nabh feels something clench deep inside. He's never seen Ajoba cry. If Ma died, what would Nabh see in the sky?

That clench gets heavy, a pressure in his chest, and he gasps. Krishna rolls over, his furry face inches from Nabh's, concern in his eyes.

"It's okay, beta." Ajoba chuckles. "An old man looks backward while a young man looks forward."

Nabh doesn't understand what Ajoba means, but he's relieved to hear Ajoba laugh. They watch the clouds for a while, calling out different shapes. Like Snoopy, Ajoba sees elaborate images, the Mahabharata War, and the Taj Mahal. Nabh is more like Charlie Brown. A horsey and a ducky.

An alarm goes off in the distance. The fire drill. In a few minutes, Kyle will probably be supergluing quarters to the ground. But suddenly, over the alarm, pop pop pop, like stepping on sheets of bubble wrap. At first, Nabh thinks it's Kyle, doing a different prank. But the alarm and the popping feel wrong somehow. Something is wrong.

Nabh's heart is pounding hard. He and Ajoba sit up. Just as they look toward the school, the sky over it erupts with bursts of clouds: a basketball, a flip-flop, a coffee mug, LEGOs, a recorder, an open book, a jump rope, a hula hoop, a lipstick, a tie, a pair of Nikes. And, over the alarm and bubble wrap, sirens screaming louder and louder.

KALPITA PATHAK is an autistic, disabled, queer Indian-American writer. A former Michener fellow, her poetry has been published in several magazines, including *Autumn Sky Daily*, *San Pedro River Review*, *Unbroken*, and *South Dakota Review* (2025). Her fiction has been shortlisted for the SmokeLong Quarterly Award for Flash Fiction and published in *Wigleaf* and *The Massachusetts Review*.

14

Kintsugi

Sascha Sizemore

One time, a porcelain doll lived within a music box. Beautiful, everyone who saw it said, pale skin and dark hair, raised en pointe with hands brushing the sky, forever dancing in an endless twirl.

The doll was fragile; everyone knew that, but no one paid much mind. It was safe inside its music box, feet floating above its stage, spinning in time with a shower of tinkling bells. It liked being like this, or so the crowd said, liked the safety and structure. The doll never had to question what it was to do; it simply had to dance.

One chilly morning, the doll's foot slipped. It was nothing spectacular, just a simple accident. It fell as the crowd watched, between one heartbeat and the next, crashing down to hard ground, one of those eternally raised arms shattering as it took the force of the blow. The music box tinkled mockingly as the doll lay there, gasping, immobile, and staring down at where its arm had been until the bells fell silent.

—What do we do?

—I didn't know it could fall.

—Get the creator.

And so the doll's creator came, gathering up the frozen doll and all the shattered pieces of what had been. The creator took the doll to the kiln where it had been built and fired it anew, the pieces of the arm held together by molten metal. It hurt, but the doll did not scream. Not until it was back inside its music box and lifted its new white-gold arm above its head, preparing for another dance, and froze, stutter-stop still as the gold pulled and tugged, refusing to cede to anything but gravity.

—What are you waiting for? Dance, the creator demanded.

—I can't. It hurts.

Mouth pressed into a sneer colder than the doll's porcelain body, the creator turned away and started the music box again. The platform underneath the doll began to spin, and it was all it could do not to fall again, to lift its screaming golden arm and begin to twirl. But the doll obeyed. It knew nothing else. It wobbled, it shuddered, but it danced.

The next fall came two weeks later. Exhausted from fighting its arm, the doll lowered it and fell victim to its uncertain gravity, snapping both perfectly extended legs below the tutu. Again, the crowd called, and again the creator came, muttering expletives and snarling malice as the doll's pieces were gathered up and returned to the kiln. This time, the doll screamed as gold was poured into its legs, as the gold in its arm burned in time with the crackles of the fire.

Be quiet. I didn't make you scream.

When the music box was again in sight, the doll tried to stand, but the lightning that tore up through its legs into its very core was too much, arms and legs throbbing in unison. The doll wanted to fold back down, to curl up like a wounded animal and breathe until the pain was gone. It knew that would be what those witnesses to its dance would do if they hurt like this, but the doll was not made to be one of them. It was made to entertain them. And so, painted face contorted into a grimace, it stepped back up onto the platform. It danced.

It danced, and the crowd watched, but they grumbled now. The doll didn't look pretty with its face like that, with the tears beading in its eyes. The gold shining in its cracks glowed under the sunlight, but that served only as a reminder. It was slower now, cautious. No longer did its head lift towards the sky, ethereal, closer to flight than dance; it watched its feet carefully, determined not to slip. What is the point of this, they muttered among themselves. They were here for a performance, not a prayer.

The rock came from no one and everyone, flung from the crowd, anonymous and half understood and inexorably, brutally real all the same. It hadn't stopped, exactly, just slowed for a heartbeat to breathe. The missile caught the doll dead in the face in an explosion of ceramics and one haunting music note. Yet again, the crowd stood, grumbling, waiting for the show they had come to expect as the doll's pieces were hauled away and it was brought back, thrashing, a mask of gold sealed over its once-beautiful face, moaning uselessly as it was deposited upon its stage.

The platform began to turn.

SASCHA SIZEMORE is a deafblind author and poet chronicling life and the dark things that slip through the cracks. After receiving a BFA in creative writing from the University of North Carolina Wilmington, he can be found at work on his debut novel alongside his guide dog Marigold, usually with coffee in hand and music playing.

15

The Bride Is Eating Cake and the DJ Is Playing Werewolves of London

Andrew Stancek

The couple at the next table has brought a three-year-old to the wedding reception. Martha sports a pinched look, but we do not speak. Words have failed us. The child's mother pours herself a third refill from the bottle of red; the father devours a shrimp cocktail. Their eyes tick everywhere except towards their bundle of joy, Myles, who careens from table to table, tugs on table cloths, shrieks, wiggles out of embraces. He knocks over two wine glasses and a vase; his parents fail to notice. The free bar, I was pleased to discover, serves Brut and Stolichnaya vodka.

THE MEN'S FORMAL wear market is on life support. Curly, my boss, has waved goodbye to three of his fellow regional managers, reigns as a newly-minted capo dei capi. On Thursday, he called me into his office, overflowing with sale shirts and ties, for a warning.

"A layoff is coming. You'll need to double your sales."

His shaved head gleamed; the missing eyebrows reinforced his look of a wannabe wrestler.

ZEN EMPHASIZES SELF-RESTRAINT and insight into the mind. In the Flower Sermon, Buddha holds up a flower, wordlessly, and Mahākāśyapa smiles, understanding. I practice chants, breathe *Om*, dismiss impatience. Large gatherings, throbbing with jollity and relatives' disapproval, remain a challenge. I close my eyes, inhale.

MARTHA AND I ended our happy union two weeks ago, eighteen months after our own exuberant wedding. On Wednesday, on the phone, she sizzled: We committed, I absolutely will not go to a wedding alone, I will *not* tell Hilary, my lifelong friend, that you and I have split. You'd better suck in your gut and spend one more evening of your precious life with me. The chicken we just ate was drier than the Sahara and the carrot mush I could serve to Myles, if anyone ever catches him. He rolls on the dance floor, trips dancers, wails as a burly man snags him. Gifted with a frothy strawberry concoction, he pipes down and slurps.

I STARTED OUT selling jackets, tuxes, cummerbunds, and sus-penders in my father's store, as soon as I turned fourteen. Every weekend, I flashed smiles with a measuring tape around my neck, pins in my mouth, ready for alterations. Going home on the subway, I'd classify every man, standing or sitting: 34 short, 44 tall, 50 extra tall. I learned hemming at eighteen. When Father sold his store to the chain, he told me I was set for life, that suits will never go out of style, that there'll always be weddings. He died basking on a Florida golf course, better off not knowing about a pandemic, about weddings in polo shirts and shorts. Curly used to sell car parts, muscled his way up to management, through a connection to the conglomerates that preside over assorted retail businesses. To him a sixteen and a half and a seventeen neck is all the same.

THE MEDITATOR, IN Hongzhi's practice, strives to be aware of the totality of phenomena, instead of focusing on a single object, learns to cultivate the empty field. In Japan, a follower can blow Zen by playing a shakuhachi bamboo flute. I have savings: once I leave behind Curly and pleated bib shirts, I will fly to Takahama.

THE VOLUME OF the music has increased; the lights have dimmed. The woman Martha is talking to has a wandering eye, gives me an "I'll give you my phone number" look. The DJ has put on "Wasn't That A Party," much too soon. Everything is happening too soon. I'm not thirty anymore. This morning, I could not zip up my black pants; instead of a session with my sensei, I rushed to the mall in search of a better fit.

We should have had a baby. We should have tried harder. We should have slowed down the merry-go-round.

I exhale, center, lead Martha to try a new dance.

ANDREW STANCEK has been published widely, in *SmokeLong Quarterly, Frigg, Cleaver, Funicular, Hobart, Green Mountains Review, Boston Literary Magazine, New World Writing Quarterly, The Hong Kong Review,* and *New Flash Fiction Review,* among others. He has won the London

Independent Story Prize contest, the Reflex Fiction contest, the New Rivers Press American Fiction contest, and has been nominated for the Pushcart Prize. His novella-in-flash, entitled *Saying Goodbye*, was published in 2023.

16

Birds

Laura Theis

I.

You are still little, and your neighbor has a cat called Moonface.
An impossibly beautiful creature, all languor and white fluff and huge beryl eyes, and yet, as should be expected of her kind, a sadist and a killer.

Moonface is in the habit of decorating the edge of the decking with small dead bodies, half-chewed pieces of voles and frogs and dormice; now she has left a gray-and-red feather ball that had once been a baby robin. You pick it up and hold it, the softest, most delicate thing you've ever touched. You take a breath, eyes closed, little face scrunched up, and imagine that you can feel the tiniest heartbeat, faint and rapid, then a flutter between your palms. When you open your eyes, so does the robin. You look at each other for a long moment until the baby bird gives the gentlest chirp. You carry him into your bedroom and feed him blueberries and rum-soaked raisins; you will him to be alive and well with the full force of your five-year-old being until his wounds have healed and he is strong enough to rejoin his family.

II.

You are a scrawny teenager at Ruby's birthday sleepover, jumping on mattresses in neon print pajamas, telling ghost stories, and eating "midnight soup" at ten o'clock, feeling incredibly grown up. You wake up in the middle of the night, needing to pee, and traipse around the landing on tiptoes until you find the door to the unfamiliar bathroom.

Once inside, you feel around for a light switch, but, incapable of finding one, you settle for the moonlight flooding in through the skylight. You are just washing your hands when you hear a sharp click from the direction of the door—the key being turned in the lock. You had completely forgotten about locking up—none of the rooms in your own house have locks, not even the bathrooms. You turn your head and see the dark outline of a tall boy standing next to the door. Ruby's brother, Patrick.

"Sorry, I forgot to lock," you whisper. "I'll be right out of your hair."

And you try to squeeze past him and unlock the door again. He grabs your wrists.

"Not so fast, pretty bird."

"Please, Patrick…"

"Tell you what, I'll let you out if you give me a little kiss."

You try to wriggle free, but it is an unfair fight, and he just tightens his grip and laughs.

"Don't be such a killjoy, all I'm asking for is one little…"

He is interrupted by a loud thump, a high-pitched screech, and a sudden flurry of wing flaps. A large barn owl has somehow managed to fly in through the half-open skylight, and it perches on your shoulder, hooting. You feel its weight, the claws burrowing into your shoulder through the thin fabric of your pajamas, and you relax into the owl's oddly painless grip, knowing you have somehow, inexplicably, won the fight. You free your wrists and, with Patrick just standing there gaping, you unlock the door and walk out past him and back into Ruby's bedroom filled with snoring girls, your cheek pressed into the soft feathers of the savior on your shoulder. The owl stays until you fall asleep, nodding, eyes glowing amber. By the morning, it has disappeared, and Patrick gives you a glance over the breakfast table, but never says anything.

III.

You're living in the city, quite cut off from the gardens and nature and birdsong you grew up with, and begin to experiment with scavenger crows. You do it unintentionally, more as a mind-calming exercise than anything, the way other girls clutch their keys and pepper sprays in their handbags or pretend to be on the phone when walking alone in a scary neighborhood.

You walk weaponless, humming to yourself, and whenever you hear footsteps coming up behind you, you imagine a murder of crows standing guard and watching on the rooftops above.

Depending on how anxious you are, you start with as little as three and let them grow exponentially in your mind, you look up, and there they are, unfailingly, cawing to each other across power lines, as if sharing a joke.

Their presence gives you the confidence to wear what you please, to walk any route at your own pace at any time of night, head held high, breathing freely.

It does not, however, make you entirely immune to catcalls or other unwanted attention. You do not usually let the birds intervene until things are getting desperate. But that time you see a guy pull a knife out of his pocket, blade sprung open in his hand, it doesn't take more than two seconds till one of the crows has snatched it out of his grasp and flown away with it, cackling, while another three fly at him full force with claws outstretched.

IV.

Some mornings, you get up at the crack of dawn just to stand on the rooftop and color the early sky with swirling clouds of parrots and flamingos and birds of paradise. Eagles and vultures, even albatrosses.

They all come, like clockwork.

V.

The fact that you constantly surround yourself with birds doesn't draw as much attention as one might think. This is a jaded city. Your friends are all oblivious to the extent of your gift, and when one of your more observant housemates once questions you about the presence of a black swan in the bathtub or a gaggle of peacocks on the arms of the coat stand, you calmly explain that a) You are an eccentric bird enthusiast, and don't we all have our quirks? and b) The collective noun for peacock is actually "an ostentation."

VI.

Only your lover really knows about what you can do.

"What is your favorite thing about your power?" she whispers as you are lying in bed together, spooning, dozing.

"Delaying the damn dawn chorus," you yawn. "Hands down."

LAURA THEIS writes in her second language. Her exophonic work appears in *Poetry, Oxford Poetry, Magma, Rattle, Aesthetica,* and others. She was the recipient of the Society of Authors' Arthur Welton Award, the AM Heath Prize, Oxford Brookes Poetry Prize, Mogford Prize, Poets and Players Prize, Hammond House International Literary Award, the Alpine Fellowship Writing Prize, and a Forward Prize nomination. Her Elgin-Award-nominated debut *how to extricate yourself,* an Oxford Poetry Library Book-of-the-Month, has won the Brian Dempsey Memorial Prize. Her 2023 collection, *A Spotter's Guide for Invisible Things,* has won the Live Canon Collection Prize.

17

A Richter Scale for Heartbreaks

Lynn Kristine Thorsen

Jessy, at thirteen, was a serious birdwatcher and carefully cataloged his sightings. Junie, his best friend and three months his junior, fancied herself a trail interpreter. When they rode their bikes through the deep native woodlands just beyond their small town, Junie's eyes were on the ground, and Jessy's head was in the trees. He could whistle the call of any bird he spotted, and Junie mapped all the trails that ran through the deep woods. They were on the outskirts of puberty, and while they had talked about it only once when they were swimming in the deepest pool in the creek, they had agreed that they would marry when they were old enough.

Early one morning in late August, Jessy was helping with yard-work when he heard the heartfelt cry of Mrs. Mathew, a close neighbor. Her terrier, Dancer, had dashed out into the street and stopped in the path of an oncoming pickup truck. Jessy ran out into the street and grabbed the dog. He had just managed to toss the dog onto the curb when the truck hit Jessy, bouncing him off the bumper.

The only thing that can be said about Junie's grief is that it blackened the sky, caused rosebuds to drop without blooming, and created a dull but throbbing silence throughout the township. Everyone mourned Jessy. He had been an exceptional and beloved son. But even the love of his parents seemed to pale against the deep and terrible pain that settled on Junie.

Junie couldn't bear the memories of birds and trails of the woodlands, and so she kept to the dry, asphalted streets. Even there, Jessy's impression appeared on every tree, bush, and blade of grass. When she found the plans they'd made for an ant farm on her small desk, she wept over them until the paper fell apart in her hands.

It was her ancient neighbor, Mrs. Grath, who warned Junie about too much grieving for the dead. "You spend that much time thinking about those that are gone, something is going to come through that thin veil and haunt you." Mrs. Grath gave Junie a sack of warm cookies and sent her on her way.

Later that night, when Junie was staring out her bedroom window, she saw a girl in a fluttery white dress standing under the large oak tree in the backyard. The girl turned her face up toward Junie and lifted one hand in a silent wave. Then she seemed to drift like a leaf and was gone.

Thunder started up, the kind that rolls across the sky with rumbling swirls and groans. Junie watched a lightning bolt carve across the dark night, and a huge peal shook the house. Without knowing she had decided to go, she pulled on her rainboots and raincoat and stumbled out into the night, heading toward the woodlands. Once there, she returned to her childhood ways, hunting along the paths, her face to the ground until she came to the creek.

There, under the soft light of a slivered moon, Junie saw a slender figure moving through the water toward the deepest pool where Junie had swum with Jessy. The figure paused and turned around to face Junie as her white dress floated around her, swirled by small currents. A voice reached across the pond: "You should come here. The water is lovely. It's warmer than your bed, warmer than Christmas."

Junie stepped into the creek. The current tugged against her boots. She took a second step and could feel the current caressing her.

The figure reached a long arm out to Junie. "It's like warm cookies and milk." Junie started to walk forward, sensing more than understanding that the water was growing much deeper and colder. "We can walk together. Take my hand." A pale, transparent hand reached out to Junie as the current pulled hard, and her feet seemed to float above the rocky bottom of the creek. She could still hear a soft, drifting voice, "It's warmer here."

Junie took one last step into the deep current, then stumbled, and saw, more than felt, herself falling slowly through the water.

It was then that a yellow dog raced out from the bushes along the creek, barking and running along the bank. He was more puppy than dog, but even so, he jumped fearlessly into the water and swam toward the deep pool, toward Junie. He floundered in the chill water. There was a clear hoot of an owl, and then another. Junie looked up to see something soar just above her on wings that were silent and strong. She took a deep breath and tried to straighten up from the water as the current pulled against her. It was her struggles that turned her around toward the flailing, waterlogged puppy. As the owl hooted one last time, she began her hard struggle against the current. Junie fought her way through the water until she reached the puppy and could gather him up into her arms. Together, they moved slowly toward the shore and away from whatever the deep pool might have held. The dog, soon named Curry, was a mongrel puppy who would not be parted from Junie. He was her comfort during nights when thunder cracked and loneliness seeped in through the siding and roofing tiles. He was her comfort as they meandered together through the forest paths, and she whispered to him of the boy who had wandered the forest paths with her, and about the ant farm they had planned to build.

LYNN has written fiction for the entirety of her lengthy life. Her small publishing history includes short fiction in *Quarterly West, Calliope, Kansas Quarterly, Halfway Down the Stairs, Every Day Fiction,* and flash fiction in *Shacklebound Books, 101 Words,* and *Trembling with Fear.* Her collection of short fiction, *The Friends of Miss Emily Martine,* won the Utah Literature Prize and Publishing prize. Her fiction always has an unusual or speculative element. Some of them are wished for, others true.

18

Empty Bottle

Joseph V. Velaidum

She takes the empty urinal bottle from the nightstand and sets it aside quietly in a corner of the room. It was there for him to use when he couldn't make it to the bathroom. The floor creaks beneath her as she bends over to pick up the package of adult diapers she bought last week. The package makes that sharp, plasticky sound as she tears it open, and she winces.

He stirs. "What's this?" he says, voice cracked and small, barely able to get the breath to speak.

"You can't keep peeing in the bottle," she says. "I can't clean it up anymore."

He looks at the diaper she holds out to him, and then at her face. He doesn't take it. She stands there and finally sets it on the nightstand, like an offering, and goes back to her side of the bed and removes her hearing aids for the night. She is trying to help him, she tells herself, but she knows that she is not physically able to care for him anymore, and wonders if she is being selfish. If he would just try to help himself, she thinks. But the thought brings with it a thick and choking gust of guilt.

These days, she cannot sleep very much; the pain in her legs is too much, so she is half awake and watches it in slow-motion silence, against the backdrop of wafting snowflakes illuminated by a dull streetlight streaming in from outside. He tries to take the diaper off. Then he falls. She sees the fall, partially, but does not hear it. She doesn't move for a moment. It's like watching a plate fall—you watch it tip and you know how it will end. You try to reach out to catch it, but you only catch the edge, and somehow it seemingly accelerates its fall.

He has broken his hip, she knows. His second time. His voice, calling out for her, is sharp and frightened, and it cuts through her and slices something she thought she had already lost. She tells herself it isn't her fault. He's the one who got up. But she already knows how it will sound to other people. She knows he will say that he fell because she took away the bottle. She already hears the judgmental voices: Maybe if you…you might have…if only….

When the present is too jagged and sharp to hold, she has always retreated into her distant past, but finds no solace there either. She goes back to that summer when their first child was born. The Guyanese heat was so relentless it felt solid, like something you had to push through to get anywhere. The baby had been sick for days. She asked him to take her to the doctor. He had said no, it was his day off, and he wanted to buy some rum and spend the day in the cool shade drinking. He wasn't cruel when he said it, but his voice had been flat, like it was a fact too basic to question. So she went alone, carrying the baby through the sunlit streets, his little body heavy and limp in her arms. The doctor had looked at her with eyes that barely focused and told her to take the baby out for some air. She had stayed on the stoop of the doctor's office all day, sitting in the heat with the baby, her dress damp against her back, watching people come and go and not knowing what to do. Finally, her mother and sister came and told her they would all go to another doctor.

The other doctor told her, hours later, what he could see right away: "If only you had brought him to me a few hours earlier, I might have been able to save him." That sentence lodged itself inside her. She didn't even know she was carrying it, at first, like something slipped into her pocket without her noticing. It's still there, and it comes out in moments like this.

Now, waiting for the ambulance, she hears herself muttering something under her breath and realizes it is the doctor's voice: Maybe if you…you might have…if only….

When the ambulance arrives, she feels their eyes on her, the paramedics. She doesn't say anything to them, but she already knows what they are thinking. When they take him away, she gets the cleaning supplies to clean the pee. She cries as she cleans. Her back locks, her legs cramp, her arthritic hands barely able to hold the cloth. When she is finally finished, she looks at the empty bottle in the corner of the room. It's still there, after all.

JOSEPH V. VELAIDUM has only recently started writing fiction. He has completed his first novella, and the first of his stories has appeared in *West Word* and *Anansi* (where his story placed third in the Winter 2024-2025 competition). He is a professor at the University of Prince Edward Island (Canada).

19

Didn't We Realize We Were Drowning?

Linda Wastila

In those days, we woke with bedheads and foggy eyes and boggy brains, comfy in our slept-in yoga pants as we headed to the kitchen to make our pot of coffee, our go-to prop for endless hours of video conferences with others, also at home, also in yoga pants they'd slept in, mewling toddlers and barking dogs in the next room.

Those days, we positioned the computer monitor to cut off our chins so colleagues couldn't see us play Two Dots or Minecraft or stream CNN or NPR on our phones; often, we typed in the chat box, "iffy Wi-Fi," turned off the video, and did downward dogs, washed dishes in the kitchen, took shits in the loo, walked the dog in the park, or took our lunch in the garden.

Those days, we slept in bed linens upgraded to organic 800 count cotton and silk-lined weighted blankets to hug us in our dreams; we napped at our desks, on the living room couch, in hammocks on our decks, hammocks we didn't use as much as we wanted but knowing they swung gently in breezy sunshine reminded us, briefly, of longer days at the ocean serenaded by singing seagrass, the keening gulls, the clean ozonated air.

In those days, we jockeyed for sidewalk rights with runners and bikers and electric scooters; we walked fast, to get our shrinking hearts to pump again, to break a sweat, to feel the heady rush of our breath re-inhaled through masks, and then, the cool release when, safe at home, we ripped them off, gasping.

In those days, respite came when our Apple Watch chimed 5 p.m., and we replaced caffeine with Cabernet or gin-and-lime and/or a joint and sat outside in the garden or swung in that now less sunny hammock, and sometimes, something nudged our mind or heart and we wrote it down or, more likely, contemplated writing down the small thought that came unbidden, but mostly we worried about what to cook for dinner, those ceaseless meals, and because we didn't often foray into the world, we had to work with what still-good greens and proteins languished in the fridge.

Those days, when the sun circled to the other side of the earth or, rather, the earth shifted enough to leave us in darkness again, we gathered our greens and proteins into a bowl, doused them with sriracha—we craved sensation of any type—and filled our glass again and sat on the couch.

In those nights, we streamed Netflix and Hulu and Amazon Prime—we'd never realized the variety of true crime dramas and cooking competitions and murder documentaries and porn—and between the substances and the carbs and the hum of the tube, sometimes that thought would crash again against the edges of our brain and noodle through it, a slinking worm.

Those nights, we flipped to Animal Planet and ratcheted up the volume; we relished the violence of the lioness's take-down of the gazelle, the shark's feeding frenzy, the queen bee's deadly mating ritual, and our favorite episode, the one where lemmings migrate en masse across the tundra, diving from Alaskan cliffs into the solace of water smashing into rocks. After the fourteen-minute scene, we sat in silence for a moment, awed at the momentousness of the lemmings' foolish mistake, at the little creatures' persistence in going forward despite the risks of ending it all, and we wondered to ourselves, Don't they realize they're drowning? In those nights, we answered ourselves the same way—with a shrug—and we turned off the television and the lights and, with phones in hand, we mounted the stairs to our expensively sheeted beds and doom-scrolled ourselves to sleep.

LINDA WASTILA writes from her West Virginia homestead, where she tends chickens, gardens, and the people in her life. You can read her work in *The Missouri Review* (2021 Perkoff Prize winner for fiction), *The Penn Review, Epoch Literary Journal, Citron Review, SmokeLong Quarterly, Monkeybicycle, Blue Fifth Review*, and *Nanoism*, among others. In between life and pondering the meaning of it, you can find her toiling on her novels, concocting plant medicine, and giving a damn.

20

Hands

Deb Waters

I'm at a wedding in the Languedoc. It's the last weekend of September. I'm relieved the hot, cruel summer is almost over. There's a woman at the table next to mine with bleached hair and a magenta mouth. She looks like an eighties rock star. I can't take my eyes off her. She's wearing gold hoops and a purple boob tube that's so sheer it shows the contours of her uneven nipples. She took a call halfway through the vows, and now she's heckling the groom.

"What's her problem?" I say to the man beside me. He's wearing a linen suit, a fedora and trainers. He's an art director called Tim. Or Tom. I suspect we're being fixed up. She stands on her chair and gestures like a footie fan: oggy, oggy, oggy, oi oi oi. Other guests twitch and recoil, or try to outstare the remains of their cassoulet.

"Mattie? Oh, she's been like that since the baby," says Tim-Tom. When he talks, he views me from the corner of his eyes in shifty glimpses. There's a smudge of butter in his auburn beard.

"Baby?" The air is warm and weighted, it presses on my head like kneading fists.

"She dropped it."

"It?"

"A boy, I think."

I think about my own child, as unplanned as the relationship I was in, and as yearned for, both barely formed before their pitiful endings.

"What happened?" I ask.

"Dropped him onto a coffee table."

"A coffee table?"

Mattie sits down and leans back. She yells for champagne. Where the top's shifted to show her tan line, her skin looks sore and neglected.

"It was an accident," he says, as though my face suggests otherwise. "Wriggled out of her grasp and fell. Poor thing didn't stand a chance."

"Coffee table?" I'm a high-pitched echo.

"Yeah, one of those glass-top ones. It shattered, went everywhere." He mimes a bomb going off. Not glass breaking, a bomb. Boom.

"Jesus Christ, that's awful."

Mattie stands up and staggers towards the bride. A crimson-clad bridesmaid intercepts, puts an arm around Mattie's waist, and gently leads her away. Mattie's laughter sounds like mating foxes. I reach for a half-empty bottle of wine.

"Her husband left her. Blamed the drinking."

"Before or after?" I ask.

"Before or after what?"

I turn my head and use my fingertips to rub at the pain that's forming in my skull. The waiter puts crème brûlées in front of us. Tim-Tom stretches his limbs and rubs his palms together; he has hairy arms but smooth, feminine hands that look like they don't belong to him. He grabs a spoon and whacks the caramelized top; it cracks and splinters. Boom, he mimes again.

I push mine away. "You don't want it?" he says, and takes mine.

I put my elbows on the table, rest my chin on my palms, and watch Mattie. She twirls and sways to "Dancing Queen." Wary guests give her a wide berth. When "Copacabana" comes on, I drain my glass, scrape my chair back, and shimmy up to her. Mattie smiles and hugs me, though she doesn't know who I am. She smells of cigarettes and almonds. We move around in a drunken clasp, and when Tim-Tom joins us, I take those warm hands of hers in mine and lead her off the dance floor.

DEB WATERS won the Bridport Short Story Prize, and in 2024, she won *The Letter Review*'s Short Fiction competition. Debra has also been shortlisted for the Bath Short Story Award, the Bridport Flash Fiction Prize, the Oxford Flash Fiction Prize, and the Pat Kavanagh Award, and was a finalist for the London Independent Story Prize, aka LISP, (flash category) and highly commended for the Writers and Artists Working Class Writers Prize. She has been published online in *Litro*, *LISP*, *The Letter Review,* and *Flash Flood*.

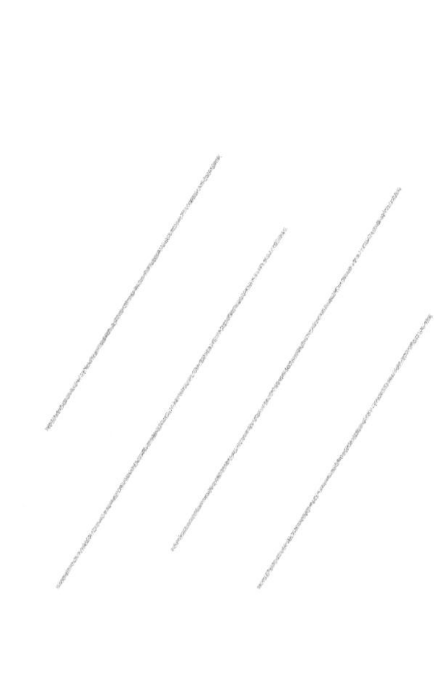